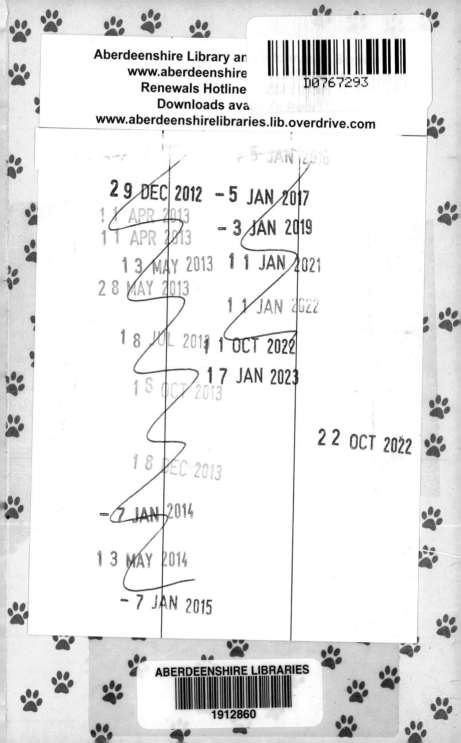

This book
belongs to

....

Puddle's Fan Pages

Here's what other children have to say about their favourite puppy and his latest adventure!

"It's funny when they make a snow Puddle using Grandad's slippers for ears."
Isabel, age 7

"Christmas Snow Puppy is my favourite Puddle story. My favourite bit was when Puddle slid on his tummy. That was really funny!" Maia, age 5

"My favourite bit was when Alfie called out the names of the huskies and lots of them were called the same names as Father Christmas's reindeer."
Caitlin, age 6

"I liked the part where the children made snow angels in the snow!"
Jasmine, age 6

"I liked this Puddle story as I liked all the snow and the huskies. My favourite part was when Puddle got the collar that jingled and jangled. That was good."
Evie, age 5

"I liked the bit when Puddle couldn't get through the puddles because they were frozen! It made me laugh!" Abby, age 5

"I really liked Puddle getting a real bone!"
Lucina, age 5

Puddle
the naughtiest puppy

Christmas
Snow Puppy

**Other books about
Puddle the Naughtiest Puppy:**

Puddle
the naughtiest puppy

Christmas
Snow Puppy

by Hayley Daze

illustrated by Rowan Clifford

cover illustrated by Paul Hardman

A catalogue record for this book is available from the British Library

Published by Ladybird Books Ltd
A Penguin Company
Penguin Books Ltd., 80 Strand, London WC2R 0RL, UK
Penguin Books Australia Ltd., Camberwell, Victoria, Australia
Penguin Group (NZ) 67 Apollo Drive, Rosedale,
North Shore 0632, New Zealand

001 –

1 3 5 7 9 10 8 6 4 2
Series created by Working Partners Limited, London W6 0QT
Text © Working Partners Ltd MMX
Cover illustration © Working Partners Ltd MMX
Interior illustrations © Ladybird Books Ltd MMX

Special thanks to Mo O'Hara

ISBN: 978-1-40930-405-0
Printed in England

Mixed Sources

Product group from well-managed
forests and other controlled sources
www.fsc.org   Cert no. SA-COC-001592
© 1996 Forest Stewardship Council

FSC

To Elizabeth and Lil for your Puddle-rrific ideas

When clouds fill the sky and rain starts to fall,
Ruby and Harry are not sad at all.
They know that when puddles appear on the ground,
A magical puppy will soon be around!

Puddle's his name, and he's the one
Who can lead you to worlds of adventure and fun!
He may be quite naughty, but he's clever too,
So come follow Puddle – he's waiting for you!

A present from Puddle:

Look out for the special code at the back of the book to
get extra-special games and loads of free stuff at Puddle's
website! Come and play at www.puddlethepuppy.com

Contents

Chapter One
Snowy Surprises

Snow squished between the fingers of Ruby's red gloves as she rolled the snowball in her hands, getting ready to take aim at her cousin Harry.

"That's not how to make a snowman," Harry said, pushing his glasses back into place. "You roll the snowball on the ground to make it bigger, like this."

"Then can I throw it?" Ruby giggled.

Harry rolled his eyes and smiled at Ruby.

"Just kidding," she said.

Ruby looked back at Grandad's cottage. It was just like the front of a Christmas card, all dusted with snow. Inside, everyone was crammed into Grandad's kitchen. Mum was making her special parsnip, peach and pistachio stuffing, and Uncle Dan, Harry's dad, was busy measuring ingredients for his eggnog trifle.

Ruby and Harry had been told to play outside as they were getting "under everyone's feet", which didn't make sense at all to Ruby. *Nobody stepped on us!* she thought.

Ruby was glad their families were spending the Christmas holidays together, but she wished there was more snow. They had used up most of the snow on the grass already, and their snowman still only came up to Ruby's knees.

"I'm just making the head into a perfect sphere," Harry said.

"I don't want a head like a spear," Ruby said.

"No, a sphere." Harry paused. "Like a football shape." He rolled it over and they lifted the snowball on to the body. Both cousins stood back and looked at their creation.

"It doesn't look much like a snowman . . ." Harry started.

"More like a snow puppy," Ruby said with a smile. "Now for some finishing touches."

Ruby grabbed an old belt from the odds and ends they had dragged out of Grandad's hall cupboard and wrapped it round the snow puppy's neck like a collar. Harry found two big black buttons to use for eyes. Then they picked up Grandad's slippers and put one on each side of the head for the puppy's ears.

"It's starting to look like someone we know," Harry said.

Ruby smiled as she remembered all the magical adventures that they had been on with Puddle, a naughty puppy who arrived whenever it rained.

Fluffy flakes of snow started fluttering to the ground around them. *I wonder if Puddle will come to see us when it snows too*, Ruby thought.

Almost as if he'd read her mind, the real Puddle scampered out from the hedge and bounded across the garden towards Ruby and Harry, slipping and sliding on the slushy snow.

"Puddle!" they shouted. "Watch

out for the . . ."

Puddle crashed into the snow puppy, sending buttons and slippers flying across the garden.

"Puddle, you naughty puppy," Harry said, wiping snow from his glasses.

Ruby squealed. "Now we can have a snowy adventure!"

"Woof, woof," Puddle barked, as

if in agreement. He shook himself
from nose to tail and raced along
the garden path. He sniffed at the
icy puddles. Then the puppy took
a running jump at one of the bigger
pools.

Splat!

Instead of jumping through it,
Puddle slid across the ice on his
tummy, spread out like a starfish.

"Oh no," Harry said. "He can't jump through the puddle if it's frozen!"

Ruby sighed. "Maybe we can't have our winter adventure after all."

Chapter Two
Slip-Sliding Away!

"Look," Harry said. "Puddle hasn't given up yet."

The puppy ran up to the next icy puddle along the path, then the next one, and the next one, slipping and sliding as he went. Finally he came to a puddle that wasn't completely frozen. He sniffed it and tapped the surface of the water with his paw.

"He's going to try to jump through it," Ruby cried, jumping up and down in excitement. "Go, Puddle!"

The puppy backed away from the melted puddle, then sprinted towards it. He leapt high into the air and splashed into the puddle, nose first. Puddle's wagging tail disappeared beneath the icy water.

"Yaaay!" Ruby shouted. She tugged on her plaits for luck and pulled her cosy bobble hat down over her ears. "Come on, Harry, let's dive in too!"

Harry pulled his coat tightly around him.

"One, two, three!" they shouted and dived into the chilly water.

Ruby and Harry landed head first in a huge snowdrift. Ruby pushed the light, fluffy snow with her arms. *It's like we're swimming inside a meringue!* she thought. Their wellies, sticking out of the drift, kicked in the air as the cousins wriggled around to turn themselves the right way up.

"Now this is what I call snow," Ruby said, smiling as she poked her head out of the snowdrift.

"This is what I call cold," Harry corrected, shaking the snow from his hat. He wrapped his scarf around his neck and helped Ruby to her feet.

The two of them looked around at the carpet of untouched white that stretched as far as they could see. It was dotted with lush green pine trees. Snowflakes fell from the cloudy sky and glistened on the ground.

"It's magical," Ruby said. A big white snowflake landed on the end of her nose, and her eyes crossed as she tried to look at it before it melted on

her skin.

"Hey, where's Puddle?" Harry asked.

Puddle's head popped out from

behind the big drift of snow. "Woof, woof," he barked, and ran up and jumped on Ruby and Harry, wagging his tail.

"We're glad to see you too, boy," Ruby said.

But Puddle kept bouncing. He yelped and pawed at Ruby and Harry's coats.

"Are you trying to tell us something, Puddle?" Harry asked.

Ruby was sure she heard a dog yelping, but this time it wasn't Puddle. "Harry, can you hear that?" she asked.

"It sounds like it's coming from over there," Harry said, pointing.

Ruby turned to see a pack of dogs pulling a sledge. A boy stood at the back of it. "Haw!" he shouted, and the dogs barked back. "Gee!" the boy yelled, and the dogs yelped.

The dogs pulled the sledge in a zigzag across the snowy ground. It was sliding faster with every turn.

The boy looked up and seemed

to spot Ruby, Harry and Puddle.
"Whoa!" he called to the dog team.
He whistled and tugged on the reins.

"They're going too fast to stop,"
Harry said.

The boy waved frantically at them
as the sledge came closer and closer.

"And they're heading straight
towards us," Ruby realized in horror.
"Quick! Jump!"

Chapter Three
Mushing Through
the Snow

Ruby scooped up Puddle. She and
Harry jumped out of the way as the
sledge raced past them. The boy was
trying to keep control of the powerful
dog team.

"Easy! Easy!" he shouted. "Whoa!"

The sledge skidded to a stop. The
dogs jumped and tumbled and the
boy tipped out into the drift. Harry,

Ruby and Puddle ran over to them.
The boy stood up and brushed the
snow off his thick green parka. He
was just as tall as Ruby and his dark
brown eyes peeked out from under
the hood of his coat.

"Are you OK?" Ruby asked.
"I'm fine," he said, digging in the

snow to try to free his sledge from the drift.

Ruby held out her hand to the boy. "Hi, I'm Ruby," she said. "This is my cousin Harry and that's Puddle."

Puddle barked as he jumped and played with the other dogs.

"I'm Alfie," said the boy, shaking her hand. "Wow, your dog is already making friends with my huskies. What kind of dog is Puddle?"

"The naughty kind," Ruby replied with a grin.

"That's Rudolph." Alfie pointed to the husky at the front of the group. "He's the best lead dog. Aren't you, boy?"

Rudolph was four times bigger than Puddle. Ruby thought that the huskies all looked like they were wearing big fluffy winter coats.

Alfie gestured to the other huskies. "These two are my point dogs, the dogs that follow Rudolph – Dasher and Dancer. And these are my wheel dogs, who make the sledge turn, Prancer and—"

"Vixen?" Ruby guessed, remembering the names of Santa's reindeer.

"No," Alfie said, and walked over to his team. "She's called Lulu."

Harry and Ruby laughed. Alfie looked at them for a moment with a serious expression, then laughed as well. Lulu yipped as Alfie scratched her behind the ear.

"My uncle names all the huskies,"

Alfie said. "He's got Vixen, Comet, Cupid, Donner and Blitzen on his team."

"Are you and your uncle both dog sledge racers?" Ruby asked. The dogs were rolling around in the snow. Ruby thought they looked like they were having fun.

"They call it 'mushing', I think," Harry corrected her.

"Is that because you mush the snow down as you go over it?" she asked.

Alfie smiled. "No, 'mush' is just a way of saying 'go'. Most mushers use a different command now, though. We yell 'hike!'"

"Like this? HIKE!" Ruby shouted.

"Oh, no!" Harry said. "I don't think you should have done that . . ."

Chapter Four
Frosty Furry Fun

The huskies all yelped and started pulling the sledge in different directions. Rudolph was pulling too, but limping on his front leg. Puddle ran up to Rudolph and barked.

"Look at Rudolph," Ruby said. "There's something wrong with his leg."

"Poor Rudolph, he must have

twisted it when we crashed," Alfie
said. "Whoa, whoa!" he called.

He caught the harnesses and
held the dogs as they calmed down.
Puddle nuzzled the huskies as Alfie
gently stroked each of them.

"Good dogs, good dogs," he

repeated softly, scratching them behind the ears.

Ruby turned to Alfie. "I'm sorry I set the dogs off by yelling 'hi . . .'" She stopped herself. "Ooops."

"It's OK. You have a good loud voice. You need that to be a musher," Alfie said.

Ruby smiled. She had always known that being able to yell across three gardens would come in handy one day.

Harry knelt down beside Rudolph. "I know some first-aid. If I wrap up his leg it'll give him some support." He took off his scarf and tied it around Rudolph's leg. "That should

make him feel better."

"He can't run, though," said Alfie with a sigh. Big flakes of snow blew around them. "How are we going to make it to the Winter Festival now?"

"Winter Festival," Ruby piped up. "That sounds like fun."

"Yeah," Alfie said, but he didn't

sound like he was happy. "It would be fun if I could find it. I was following my uncle, but then the snow started and his tracks were covered by the fresh snow. Then I ran into you – well, nearly."

"Maybe we can help," Ruby said. She grabbed hold of a low branch of a pine tree and swung her legs up.

"I need a bird's-eye view." She picked a sweet-smelling pine needle out of one of her plaits. "I'll let you know what I see from the top," she said as she scrambled up the tree.

Puddle leapt over the huskies and rolled in the snow with them.

"I can see some black dots moving around over there. Maybe they're people." Ruby pointed from the treetop. "Or they might be penguins."

"Penguins live in the Antarctic!" Alfie shouted up to her. "This is the Arctic Circle."

"There are some tents and pretty lights, too," Ruby said.

"That sounds like the place," Alfie

said. "Let's go."

Ruby climbed down the tree as Harry and Alfie unhitched Rudolph's harness and placed him in the sledge. Ruby tucked a warm blanket around Rudolph as Harry and Alfie jumped on, ready to go.

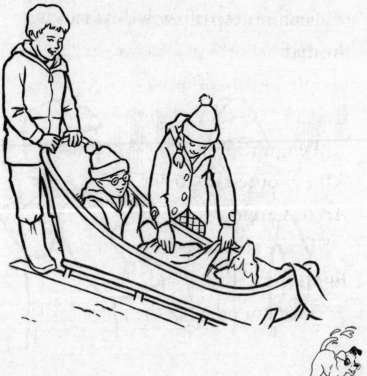

"Hang on – where's Puddle?"
Harry asked.

Ruby looked around. She could
only see white snow and pine trees,
and no sign of the naughty little
puppy.

"What's that?" Alfie said, pointing
to a small lump of snow next to
the drift.

Ruby ran over to it, calling,
"Puddle!"

The puppy burst out of the snow
pile, completely covered in snow.

"Now you look just like a real snow
puppy, Puddle." Ruby giggled.

Puddle barked and shook off
the snow.

"And now you look like a real snow girl," Harry said to Ruby.

Ruby looked down at her coat, which was covered in snow. "Puddle,

you really are a naughty puppy," she said. She brushed herself off and they both jumped on to the sledge.

"Let's go to the festival!" Ruby squealed.

"Just one thing," Alfie said. He took a collar of sleigh bells from the side of the sledge and put it on

Puddle. "Now we'll be able to hear you, even if we can't see you."

Puddle jingled his new bells as Alfie called out to the huskies. "On, Dasher! On, Dancer! On, Prancer! On, Lulu! Hike!"

This time the dogs didn't move.

"They miss Rudolph," Alfie said. "He's their leader."

"But we have to get to the festival," Harry said.

Ruby noticed the swirling sky. "And the snow is coming down hard. If we don't leave soon, we won't be able to see where we're going."

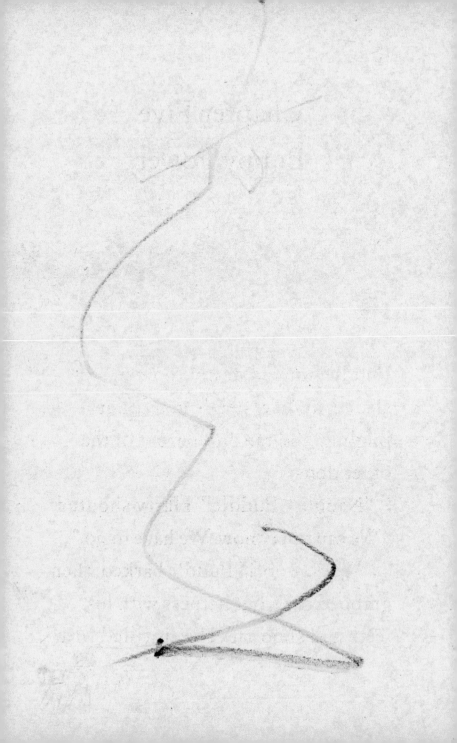

Chapter Five
Puppy Power

Puddle jumped down from the
sledge, his new sleigh-bell collar
jingling, and ran out in front of the
other dogs.

"Naughty Puddle!" Harry shouted.
"We can't play now. We have to go."

"Woof, woof!" Puddle barked, then
grabbed the front harness with his
teeth and shook it. The air filled with

the sounds of Puddle's sleigh bells.

"Puddle, leave Rudolph's harness alone," Ruby called.

Puddle wriggled about with the harness until it dropped down over his head. "Woof, woof!" he barked again. Then he yelped like the huskies had done when they were running.

"Puddle wants to be the lead dog! Can he do that?" Ruby asked Alfie.

"It's worth a try. Let's hook him up and we'll see." Alfie adjusted Rudolph's harness to fit Puddle and climbed back into the sledge.

"Are you ready to go, Puddle?" Alfie shouted.

Puddle yelped and wagged his tail.

"OK, then. HIKE! HIKE!" Alfie shouted.

This time the huskies took off like a rocket. Ruby and Harry held on tightly to the sides of the sledge. Puddle raced ahead, pulling with all

his might. His tiny legs were charging through the snow.

Rudolph whimpered at the back of the sledge.

"He wants to be down there running," Alfie said. "I'd better sit next to him so I can look after him." He slowed the sleigh. "Here, you take the reins, Harry." He handed Harry the leather straps and the boys traded places. "And you call out the commands to the team, Ruby." Alfie smiled. "You've got the voice for it."

"What do I say?" Ruby asked Alfie.

"Remember how you made them start running?" Alfie said with a grin. He pulled Rudolph close.

"*HIKE!*" Ruby shouted as loudly

as she could, for as long as her voice would let her. The dogs set off again.

After a few minutes, Alfie called to Ruby, "OK, we're coming up to a turn, so shout *GEE* to go right."

"*GEE!*" Ruby screamed at the top of her lungs, and the dogs made the turn. Harry held on tight to the reins and steered the sledge around the corner.

"Good. Now try *HAW* to go left," Alfie said.

"*HAW!*" Ruby called, and the dogs followed her command again. She turned and smiled at Alfie. "This is great!"

"It's really hard to see now," said

Harry, wiping snowflakes from his glasses with the back of his sleeve. "I think it's snowing even more heavily."

"We need to get the team to go faster," Alfie said. "You make a kind of kissing noise to do that."

"That can't be right." Ruby scrunched her face up in confusion. Was Alfie making a joke?

"Really," Alfie said. "That's what you do. Now hurry."

Ruby thought for a second and then said, "OK." She pretended she was blowing air kisses to imaginary fans.

"*Mwhaah, mwhaah, mwhaah.*"

The dogs all sped up, and Ruby, Harry and Alfie lurched backwards. The snow and the wind were stinging their faces.

"Wow, it works," Ruby sputtered through the big flakes of snow.

The snow was coming down so hard that it looked like a curtain of white in front of them.

"I can't see a thing," Harry said.

"We'd better slow down. Easy!" Alfie called.

Puddle and the dogs slowed and then stopped.

"That was really quick," Ruby said. "I didn't even get to say the 'whoa' bit."

She could hear the dogs panting as she, Alfie and Harry jumped down from the sledge. Harry stopped suddenly and tugged on Ruby's sleeve.

"What is it?" she asked.

Ruby turned to face where Harry was looking and gasped. A huge white bear was rearing up on its hind

legs, its claws stretched out above
their heads.

"A polar bear!" they screamed.

Chapter Six
Polar Adventures

"Let's mush out of here!" Ruby
hollered. "Alfie, come on!"

But Alfie and the dogs weren't
running away. And the polar bear
wasn't chasing them. It hadn't moved
at all.

Alfie laughed and tapped the bear
on its arm. "See? It doesn't bite,"
he said.

Ruby and Harry slowly walked up to the bear. Harry took off his glove and touched its front leg with his finger.

"Ice?" he said. "It's made of ice."

The snowfall eased up again and
Ruby and Harry could make out
shapes around them. Ruby could
see majestic ice eagles and swans,
powerful-looking horses and even a
huge walrus.

"Wow, they're all ice sculptures!"
Harry exclaimed.

"Welcome to the Winter Festival,"
Alfie said as he unhitched the dogs
from the sledge. "Isn't it amazing?"

"It certainly is," agreed Ruby –
then she gasped. Beyond the animal
sculptures was an ice castle. It was

as big as Grandad's cottage, but with sloping roofs and turrets with ice flags flying from the tops. Ruby imagined herself standing in the ice tower dressed as a snow queen.

"Did someone carve all of these sculptures?" Harry asked.

"Not just one person," Alfie explained. "Lots of us do ice sculpting for the Winter Festival. This year my uncle and I have been asked to show our work for the first time. It's a great honour."

Alfie stopped and waved at someone. Ruby turned and saw a man dressed in a parka just like Alfie's. He was chiselling away at an ice

sculpture of a team of huskies pulling
Santa's sledge. He ran his hand across
the curled runner of the sledge, then
looked up at Alfie and waved.

"That's Uncle Jack," Alfie said. "Come and meet him!"

They ran over. Uncle Jack put down his chisel and gave Alfie a hug. "Alfie, there you are. I was getting worried. And you've brought some friends."

"Yes," Alfie said and put an arm around each of his new friends. "This is Ruby and Harry."

Puddle barked and jingled as he chewed Uncle Jack's trouser leg.

"And that naughty puppy is Puddle – the newest lead dog in the Arctic Circle," Alfie added.

Uncle Jack shook Ruby and Harry's hands and patted Puddle on the head. "They are going to open

the festival soon," he said. "We have to finish our sculpture." He handed Alfie a chisel and a hammer. "I've saved the lead dog for you to do."

Alfie took the tools and walked over to the husky-sized block of ice at the front of the other carved dogs in the team.

"Can we help?" Ruby asked.

"Sure, you can polish the sections that Uncle Jack has finished," Alfie said. "That would be a big help."

Ruby and Harry collected some polishing cloths from Uncle Jack.

Puddle jumped on top of the block of ice and started to lick it.

"It looks like Puddle wants to help, too," Harry said.

Alfie quickly chipped with his chisel and shaved the rounded corners of the sculpture. Ruby and Harry polished away, but with Puddle jumping on the ice and licking it, the block was getting smaller and smaller.

"Down, Puddle!" Ruby said. "You're making the ice melt." Puddle hopped down and scampered off, jingling all the way.

Alfie stopped chiselling and looked at the melting ice. "It's already too small to be a husky," he said. "My uncle's worked so hard on the other dogs – but without a lead dog, the sculpture will be ruined."

Chapter Seven
Still as a Statue

"We can't give up," Ruby said.
She spotted Puddle circling the
sculptures with his sleigh-bell collar
jingling. He looked like he belonged
on Santa's sleigh.

"That's it!" Ruby shouted. "Puddle
could be in the ice scene with Santa!"

"What do you mean?" Alfie asked.

"Well, Puddle pulled the sledge

with the real huskies, so maybe an ice Puddle could pull the sledge with the ice huskies," Ruby suggested.

"Yes," Harry said, measuring the smaller ice block with his hands. "The ice is still big enough to carve a Puddle-sized lead dog."

"Let's do it," Alfie said. "But I don't know Puddle well enough to carve him from memory like I do with my own dogs. He'll have to pose for me."

Ruby raced around trying to catch the cheeky puppy. "That's not going to be easy."

"It's a shame we don't have a juicy bone to give Puddle. That would keep him still," Harry said.

"One dog bone coming up," Alfie said, chiselling away at a spare bit of ice on the ground. After only a few minutes he held up a perfectly carved ice bone. "Puddle, come and get it!"

Puddle bounded over and sat by Alfie, waiting for his treat. "Woof, woof!"

"He looks happy to sit there now," Ruby said as Puddle licked the bone.

Alfie looked back and forth between Puddle and the ice block. Ruby and Harry handed Alfie tools as he carved. He used a flat chisel for the nose, an ice pick for the teeth and a small saw for the tail. He was careful but quick as he worked.

"It's finished," Alfie said with a sigh as his uncle came up and put his hand on Alfie's shoulder.

"The lead dog looks great!" Uncle Jack said. "And just in time, too."

People had started to arrive at the festival. Everyone who walked by Uncle Jack and Alfie's sculpture said how lifelike all the dogs looked, especially the little puppy at the front. Puddle sat proudly next to the statue of himself.

"Remarkable!" said a lady in a thick wool coat as she stared at the ice Puddle and then the real Puddle. "Your ice dogs look so real you expect them to bark."

Puddle leapt up into the air, jingling his bells and shaking the snow off his coat. "Woof, woof!"

The lady gasped and then smiled at Uncle Jack and Alfie. They all laughed together.

"You naughty puppy," Ruby said to Puddle as she ruffled his ears.

"Everyone loves your ice sculpture," Harry said to Alfie. "I'm sure they'll want you at the Winter Festival next year too."

"We'll just have to do a sculpture that's as full of surprises as this one," Alfie said, patting Puddle on the head.

Puddle barked and tried to run in circles around Ruby and Harry. But the icy ground was so slippery that his paws slid out from under him. He ended up spinning on his tummy – just as he had in Grandad's garden.

"Oh no," Ruby said. "If Puddle can't run in circles around us, then we won't be able to get home."

"And we won't get to eat my dad's eggnog trifle!" Harry said.

"We have to get back," Ruby said, "but how?"

Chapter Eight
Happy Holidays

"Maybe I can help you." Alfie went over to his sledge and pulled out a tiny set of leather moccasins. "We sometimes used them on the huskies when they were puppies. They give the dogs a better grip on frozen lakes."

Ruby tried the little dog slippers on Puddle and he started to run

around the cousins straight away
without slipping. "Woof, woof!"

"Thanks, Alfie. I think he likes
them," Ruby said.

"I guess it's time to go," Harry said.

Alfie nodded. "Goodbye and
thanks for everything."

Puddle barked to Alfie, then
yowled loudly to the huskies. They

howled back in reply.

"Looks like Puddle has made some good dog friends on this trip," Ruby said.

The snowy world started to go fuzzy as Puddle ran faster around them. The snowflakes sparkled and whirled through the air, and Ruby got that tingly feeling in her tummy and her toes. They were heading home!

Ruby and Harry landed in
Grandad's garden, on a patch of
untouched fluffy white snow. They
lay there on their backs, looking up at
the flakes gently falling from the sky.

"I wish I could make amazing ice sculptures," Harry said.

Ruby's eyes brightened. "Hey, I know what we *can* make," she said, stretching out her arms and legs and moving them up and down through the snow. "Snow angels!"

Harry laughed and did the same.

They stood up and looked down at where they had been lying and saw two perfectly formed snow angels.

"I wish Puddle was here to make a puppy angel with us," Ruby said.

"Hey, where is Puddle?" Harry asked.

"Puddle! Puddle!" they called out.

Ruby and Harry searched the garden, but there was no sign of him. Then Ruby looked over to where their snow puppy had been before Puddle had crashed into it.

"Harry, look!" she shouted. The snow puppy had been magically remade. It had the button eyes and slipper ears. Ruby thought it even had a cheeky look on its face, just like the real Puddle when he did something naughty.

"And look what he's wearing," Harry said. The sleigh-bell collar that Alfie had given Puddle was decorating the snow puppy's neck, and the little moccasins were on his paws.

Grandad's voice echoed across the garden, "Ruby! Harry! Dinner time!"

"Oh well, I guess we'll see Puddle next time it rains," Ruby said.

"Or snows," Harry added.

The cousins headed into the cottage, peeling off their scarves, hats, gloves and coats, dropping them to the floor as they ran to the dining room. As they reached the doorway they heard a "Woof, woof!" coming from the rug by Grandad's chair.

"Puddle!" they both cheered. They ran over and hugged the cheeky puppy.

There was a plate for Puddle by the table, and on the plate was a big juicy bone with a bright red ribbon tied around it.

Ruby smiled as she looked around the table at Mum, Dad, Uncle Dan and Auntie Margaret with baby Sarah on her lap, playing peek-a-boo under her napkin.

"Holidays are for spending with family and friends," Grandad called as he entered from the kitchen with a big roast turkey in his hands. "That means furry friends, too."

102

Can't wait to find out
what Puddle will do next?
Then read on! Here is the first
chapter from Puddle's tenth
adventure, Star of the School ...

Puddle
the naughtiest puppy

Star of the School

"Come on, Hawkeye Harry!" Ruby cried, cradling a bulging pink water balloon in her hands. "Let's see if you're as quick on the draw as Rodeo Ruby!"

It was a boiling hot day, and Ruby and her cousin Harry were in the garden behind Grandad's cottage. Harry was struggling to tie a knot in the top of his plump green water balloon. He looked at Ruby over the top of his glasses.

"In the Wild West," Harry said, "a shootout starts with the cowboys back to back. I read it in a book. They step nine paces away from each other, then on the tenth step, they turn and fire."

"Showdown time!" Ruby declared, standing with her back to Harry's.

"One, two, three . . ." The two cousins paced away from each other, counting in unison. "Eight, nine . . . TEN!"

They turned and threw the water balloons at each other.

Splat! The pink balloon burst on Harry's bare legs.

Splosh! The green balloon came down on Ruby's head.

"Rodeo Ruby has the fastest balloon in the West!" Ruby spluttered, shaking water off her plaits. The shower of water felt lovely and fresh.

"Hawkeye Harry hits the target better." Harry grinned as he polished his glasses on his T shirt. "That was a bull's-eye!"

"Refill!" Ruby giggled. She took a handful of empty water balloons out of her pocket, chose a blue one, and pulled its rubbery neck over the spout on Grandad's huge watering can. She held on to it as Harry tipped up the heavy metal can. Soon the blue water balloon was fat and wobbly. Ruby pulled it off the spout and tied it. They filled more and more balloons, until the watering can was empty.

"Let the shootout begin!" Ruby announced. They turned back to back, counted ten steps, and then they turned and hurled the water balloons at each other.

Splat! Splosh! Splat! Splat! Splat!

Soon, Ruby and Harry were soaked through and laughing so much it was hard to stand.

"We've made puddles all over the path," Ruby gurgled. "Grandad will think it's been raining!"

Plip! A ring appeared in one of the puddles. *Plip, plip.*

There was a roll of thunder in the distance.

Ruby looked at Harry.

"It is raining!" She squealed in delight as warm raindrops plopped down around them. Whenever it rained, Puddle the naughty puppy appeared, and they went on magical adventures together.

"Woof! Woof!" A bark echoed from inside Grandad's empty watering can, and a cheeky little furry head popped out.

"Puddle! How did you get in there?" Ruby pulled out the little puppy and set him down next to her on the path.

Puddle's tail wagged and wagged. Then he ran to the biggest puddle on the path, looked over his shoulder at Ruby and Harry . . . and jumped in. There was a big splash as he disappeared.

Ruby and Harry grinned at each other, and in they jumped, too.

***

To find out what happens next,
get your copy of
STAR OF THE SCHOOL!
Coming soon ...

Magic Mayhem

Ruby and Harry are amazed to find
themselves in a medieval castle . . .

. . . when Puddle
takes them
on a magical
adventure! They
meet a magician's
apprentice who is in
deep trouble. He's
lost his spell book.
Can Puddle save
the day?

Find out in MAGIC MAYHEM . . .

Pirate Surprise

Can you imagine what it's like to sail on a pirate ship?

Ruby and Harry find out – when Puddle takes them on an amazing adventure on the high seas! Captain Redbeard has a bad case of the hiccups! Will Puddle be able to cure him?

Find out in PIRATE SURPRISE…

Animal Antics

Join Puddle, Ruby and Harry
at the Safari Rescue Park!

All the animals
have problems they
need to overcome
before they can be
released into the
wild. Will Puddle
be able to help the
monkey who can't
climb?

Find out in ANIMAL ANTICS...

Puddle
the naughtiest puppy

Star of the School

Join Puddle, Ruby and Harry on their new adventure in the Wild West!

Lil the littlest cowgirl is told she is too small to join the cowboy school. But with Puddle's help, can she prove herself by catching Outlaw Pete?

Find out in STAR OF THE SCHOOL…

Puddle
the naughtiest puppy

Holiday Musical

Go on an amazing Hollywood adventure
with Ruby, Harry and Puddle!

The children are
thrilled when they
get to star in a new
movie. But the
director thinks
Puddle has stolen
the script! How can
Puddle show he's
not to blame?

Find out in HOLIDAY MUSICAL...

Christmas Special

Hi! It's Ruby and Harry again with Puddle the puppy ... and we are very excited because it's Christmas time! Aren't you?! This time of the year is magical – there's so much fun to be had with your family at home!

But sadly our friends at **Dogs Trust** have reminded us that there are many dogs out there that will not have a happy home to go to.

Dogs Trust know all about these poor dogs, as they are the UK's largest dog welfare charity and they constantly work towards the day when all dogs can enjoy a happy life in a loving home ... but there is so much more to be done. So they are asking all dog lovers like you to help!

Always remember, Puddle is a magical dog, while real dogs and puppies are living animals who need a lot of care, love and attention.

Getting a Dog:

• It is so important to remember and tell your friends and family that getting a dog as your family pet is a big commitment for everyone as they need a lot of love, care and attention.

• Dogs are wonderful pets, but as Dogs Trust say: "A dog is for life, not just for Christmas". What do you think this means?

• A family should think long and hard before getting a dog, as they are not toys or magical pets like Puddle the puppy!

• Can you see why it is not a good idea to give a puppy as a Christmas present? And now can you think of what would be great presents to give and receive?

Congratulations – you now know that a dog is for life, not just for Christmas! Next time join us to learn about the benefits of having a dog.

Remember, "A dog is for life, not just for Christmas®"
Dogs Trust has 18 Rehoming Centres around the UK and Ireland. To find out more please go to:
www.dogstrust.org.uk
For more fun and games please go to:
www.learnwithdogs.co.uk

DogsTrust

Snowy Jigsaw!

Look carefully at the picture of Ruby and Harry opposite. It has several pieces missing. Can you work out where each jigsaw piece should go?

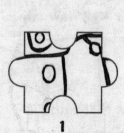

1

2

3

4

5

A Muddle of Puddles!

Look closely at the pictures of Puddle.
Can you work out which two puppies
are exactly the same?

C

D

E

F

Answers on the next page

Answers to Puddle Puzzles:
Snowy Jigsaw: 1 - D, 2 - A, 3 - E, 4 - B, 5 - C
A Muddle of Puddles: A and E are exactly the same

For more magical adventures,
come and play with Puddle at

www.puddlethepuppy.com

Use this special code to get
extra special games and free
stuff at puddlethepuppy.com

COLLAR